McLeod, Emilie
Warren

The bear's bicycle

DATE			

The Bear's Bicycle

The Bear's Bicycle

by

EMILIE WARREN McLEOD

Illustrated by

DAVID McPHAIL

An Atlantic Monthly Press Book
Little, Brown and Company
BOSTON   TORONTO

Other books by Emilie Warren McLeod

THE SEVEN REMARKABLE BEARS

CLANCY'S WITCH

ONE SNAIL AND ME

Other books by David McPhail

THE BEAR'S TOOTHACHE

OH NO GO

THE CEREAL BOX

Second Printing

T 05/75

Library of Congress Cataloging in Publication Data

McLeod, Emilie Warren.
  The bear's bicycle.

  "An Atlantic Monthly Press book."
  SUMMARY: A boy and his bear have an exciting bicycle ride.
  [1. Bicycles and bicycling — Fiction] I. McPhail, David M., ill. II. Title.
PZ7.M22496Be3   [E]   74-28282
ISBN 0-316-562033

ATLANTIC—LITTLE, BROWN BOOKS
ARE PUBLISHED BY
LITTLE, BROWN AND COMPANY
IN ASSOCIATION WITH
THE ATLANTIC MONTHLY PRESS

*Published simultaneously in Canada
by Little, Brown & Company (Canada) Limited*

PRINTED IN THE UNITED STATES OF AMERICA

For Stuart M.
and to Sally L.

Every afternoon we go bike riding.

I check the tires   and the brakes
and make sure the handlebars turn.

Then I get on my bike and coast down the driveway.
At the end of the driveway I look to the right and to the left.

I make the hand signal for a right turn and I turn right.

If I have to cross the street I stop and get off my bike.
I look both ways.
If no cars are coming I walk my bike across the street.

11

I watch for car doors that are open.

13

I steer around cans and broken glass.

I stop for dogs to make sure they are friendly.

16

When I meet another bike I stay to the right.

19

And when I come up behind people I warn them
so they can get out of the way.

When I go down a hill I don't go too fast

and I use my brakes.

I always start home before it is dark

and put away my bike.

I wipe my feet before going in the house.

Then we have milk and crackers.